Cackle Goes A-Courting

by Mecka Lind
illustrated by Lars Rudebjer

Carolrhoda Books, Inc./Minneapolis

O*nce Upon A Time* in Sweden,
there was a young and very handsome
rooster called Cackle. He lived with an
old and oh-so-very poor woman named
Mother Tilda. Their house was so
ramshackle and rickety that not even the
wind dared to sigh when it blew near.
And every letter that came was just
another bill.

   Still, neither of them could think
of living anywhere else in the world.

But one morning, Cackle woke up feeling miserable. His head hung low. His proud, red crest drooped. His shiny, feathers looked like scraggly brush.

He couldn't even get up to crow his seven-o'clock cock-a-doodle-doo.

"I know what your problem is," said Mother Tilda. "You need a wife. But I can't afford to buy you one."

"Then I guess I'll just have to go out into the world to find myself one," said Cackle. But he had lived with Mother Tilda ever since he was a little chick, so he had no idea what a wife should look like.

"She should have a proud and beautiful crest, just like yours," explained Mother Tilda.

So Cackle went a-courting to find himself a wife. He walked on down the road to a hot-dog stand. A funky-looking girl with blazing red hair was there eating a hot dog.

"That's a grand crest you've got!" Cackle said admiringly.

"You think so?" the girl asked.

"Oh, yes," Cackle said. "I'm sure Mother Tilda would like it. Would you come home with me so she could have a look at it?"

"That ought to be cool," she said. "Nothing's happening here."

When they got near the falling-down house, Cackle crowed so loudly some shingles let loose. "I've found myself a wife," he sang.

Mother Tilda looked at the girl, and the girl looked back. Then they laughed so hard they had to sit down to breathe.

"She's certainly got a grand crest, Cackle," Mother Tilda squeezed out between chuckles, "but she's a girl, not a hen. A hen is an animal, not a human being."

So Cackle went a-courting a second time to find himself a wife. He walked on down the road, past the hot-dog stand, and into a field with a mud hole. Some pigs were there, grubbing in the sludge. The biggest and most dazzling pig winked at him.

Cackle had never seen a finer animal, that's for sure. "Would you like to come home with me and live with Mother Tilda? She is oh-so-very poor, but awfully kind to animals."

"Does she like Christmas ham?" the pig grunted.

"No, I'm afraid she doesn't," Cackle sighed, worried that he had lost his new wife. "She only eats vegetables."

"Splendid!" squealed the delighted, dazzling pig.

As the rooster and the pig ambled toward the house, Cackle crowed as he had never crowed before. "Cock-a-doodle-doo! I've got myself a wife!"

This time Mother Tilda laughed even more than before, if that's possible. "It's true she's an animal, my dear Cackle," Mother Tilda giggled, "but she's a pig, not a hen. A hen is a bird—just like you!"

The dazzling pig gave an insulted grunt and waddled away.

So Cackle went a-courting a third time. He walked on down the road, past the hot-dog stand, past the field with the mud hole, and up to a pond. The lovely lady goose swimming in the pond was, without question, a bird. But just to be safe, Cackle asked, "Are you a bird?"

"Yes, of course," honked the goose. "What did you think I was?"

"Would you like to come home with me and live with Mother Tilda?" Cackle asked. "She is oh-so-very poor, but awfully kind, and she has a special liking for birds."

The lovely lady goose didn't have to think long. St. Martin's Eve was only a few weeks away, and in Sweden people can hardly dream of anything nicer than having a goose in the pan on this holiday.

Mother Tilda did not laugh when Cackle came strutting home with his beautiful goose. She had begun to feel sorry for her little rooster. "She certainly is a bird and lovely to boot," Mother Tilda said kindly, "but she's a goose, not a hen. A hen can't swim."

Cackle sighed, but he had no intention of giving up this easily.

So Cackle went a-courting a fourth time. He walked on down the road, past the hot-dog stand, past the field with the mud hole, past the pond, and into a forest. Swooping around was a sophisticated crow, doing one stunt after another. She's most definitely a bird, Cackle thought, and she doesn't look like she can swim. But to be absolutely positive, he asked, "Can you swim?"

"Swim?" she called as she dive-bombed toward him, "What need have I to swim?"

"Then would you like to come home with me to Mother Tilda's place?" he asked, taking a step back. "She likes birds who can't swim best of all, and we can stay in her warm kitchen the whole winter."

The sophisticated crow did not need to be pressed. She was already feeling a bit of a chill. She flew ahead of Cackle all the way to Mother Tilda's.

"You're coming closer!" Mother Tilda said, so as not to hurt Cackle's feelings. "She is a bird, and I doubt she can swim. But she's a crow, not a hen. A hen can't fly—only flutter. And don't forget, a hen has a crest on her head."

Cackle had forgotten. He sulked a bit, but then pulled himself together. He did want a wife.

So Cackle went a-courting a fifth time. He walked on down the road, past the hot-dog stand, past the field with a mud hole, past the pond, past the forest, and into the Big City. He strolled up one street and down another. Never before had he seen so many new and strange things. But he didn't see any hens.

Suddenly, he heard something that made him stop on the spot. It was chirping, it was flapping, it was clucking all at once. And it came out of a door that was just a little ajar.

Did he dare go inside?

Yes.

If he wanted a wife, he couldn't afford to be a coward.

Lars Rudebjers St.

Inside the door was a pet shop, where a pretty Polly parrot was sitting on a perch. She was all white and had a stunning yellow tuft on her head.

Cackle started to ask his questions right away. "Can you swim?"

"Swim!" squawked the terrified Polly. "I almost faint at the thought."

"Can you fly then?" he asked.

"Why, no," sighed Polly sadly. "My wings have been clipped. All I can do is flutter a little. Like this!"

And the pretty Polly parrot fluttered to Cackle, who was ever so happy.

"Would you mind coming home with me to Mother Tilda's place?" he sang out. "She is oh-so-very poor, but awfully kind."

The pretty Polly parrot did not mind at all, because she was quite fed up with sitting in the pet shop day after day.

"Now, Mother Tilda, she's here at last!" Cackle crowed when they arrived. "She's beautiful, and she can neither swim nor fly—only flutter. And she's got something grand on her head."

"You're right so far," said Mother Tilda, "but she is a pretty Polly parrot, not a hen." Mother Tilda was getting worried about her determined little rooster.

So she carried him into her bedroom and put him in front of the big, old cracked mirror. "Take a good look," she said.

"So that's a hen!" cried Cackle with absolute delight. "My wife is stunning!"

"My darling little nitwit," sighed Mother Tilda. "That's you you're looking at. But a hen *does* look like you. Her feathers just may not be as colorful."

"Then I know exactly," said Cackle.

So Cackle went a-courting one last time. He walked on down the road, past the hot-dog stand, past the field with the mud hole, past the pond, past the forest, and past the Big City to a stand of trees near a farm. There he met an old fox, sitting on a stone and crying. Cackle knew he shouldn't talk to a fox, but the poor old boy looked so sad, Cackle just had to ask, "Why are you crying?"

"Because the hens are so miserable I don't have the heart to steal them," the old fox sniveled. "And they aren't a bit tasty either."

"Did you say HENS?" Cackle trumpeted. "Hens that have grand crests, cannot fly or swim, only flutter, and look a lot like me? Have you seen any of those?"

"A whole barn full," howled the fox, pointing to the farm.

"Do you think there might be just one little hen who would like to come to Mother Tilda's place to peck at worms and be my wife?" Cackle gabbled.

The old fox stared at the excited rooster. "Looking for a wife, you say? And you aren't planning on living in a coop? You and your wife are going to get big and fat on good old worms?"

Cackle nodded eagerly, his brilliant crest bobbing up and down.

"Then meet me at midnight," the old fox said. "We'll see that you get your wife, don't you worry!" Then he added in a whisper, "Just make sure you all get good and plump."

They made a strange pair—the young rooster and the old fox.
But at twelve o'clock sharp, when the full moon was shining,
Cackle and the old fox stole into the big barn.

Then, for the very first time in his life, Cackle stood face-to-face
with a hen.

Well, not exactly one.

At least three hundred chickens stared at him, and he stared back. Why, they had hardly any feathers at all!

"They aren't so pretty now," whispered the fox. "But that's because they're locked in those cages. They get so crabby, they pick at each other till they lose their feathers."

Hallelujah! Cackle thought. Feathers or no feathers, they're hens just the same! He cleared his throat and crowed with joy: "Cock-a-doodle-doooo! I've come to find myself a wife. Would any one of you like to come home with me to Mother Tilda's? She is oh-so-very poor, but awfully kind."

"How many chickens live in each cage?" one voice cheeped.

"Mother Tilda can't afford a cage," Cackle said slowly. "You'll just have to scratch on the ground and stay warm with Mother Tilda and me in the kitchen during the long, cold winter."

"What's that, the ground?" another voice chirped.

"There, you see," groaned the fox. "They don't even know what the ground is. They've been cooped up all their lives."

"Then it's about time they got out," Cackle said. He called to the chickens, "Those of you who want to join me are welcome to," and the old fox opened the cages. The chickens eyed the fox suspiciously.

Cackle paid no attention. He ruffled up his feathers to look as handsome as possible. Then he strutted out of the barn with a triumphant "COCK-A-DOODLE-DOO!"

But not a hen followed him. Cackle walked on down the road in the moonlight, all alone. This is the last time I go a-courting, he thought wearily. If not a single one of those miserable hens wants me to be her husband, then I'll just have to remain a bachelor.

A little way down the road, he heard some noise behind him. One little hen came fluttering along, flapping her ragged wings as best she could.

The next morning as the sun came up, Mother Tilda stood yawning on the porch. Suddenly, she got stuck in the middle of a yawn and stared.

Cackle came strutting toward the house with a whole flock of hens and a bunch of small roosters following him. "Cock-a-doodle-doo, will these do?" Cackle crowed proudly.

"They'll do, my little Cackle," Mother Tilda said when she got over the shock. "But they are indeed the most miserable chickens I've seen in all my life. Start teaching them right now how to scratch and peck properly."

From that very first day, the chickens just got livelier and fatter on the grounds of Mother Tilda's ramshackle farm. In a whirl of happiness, they cackled and scratched, and the hens layed one egg after the other.

There were so many eggs about the place that every Saturday Mother Tilda had to bring some to town to sell. She called them *Free-Range Hens' Eggs*, because those hens certainly had free range of her little house and garden. Soon Mother Tilda was not oh-so-very poor anymore. But she still was awfully kind.

This edition first published
1992 by Carolrhoda Books, Inc.
All rights to this copy reserved
by Carolrhoda Books, Inc.

Original edition published in 1991 by
Bonniers Juniorforlag, Stockholm,
under the title TOCKEN AR LOS.
© 1991 by Mecka Lind
English language rights arranged
by Kerstin Kvint Literary and
Co-Production Agency.

Library of Congress
Cataloging-in-Publication Data

Lind, Mecka, 1942-
  [Tocken är lös, English]
  Cackle goes a-courting/by
Mecka Lind; illustrated by
Lars Rudebjer.
     p.   cm.
  Translation of: Tocken är lös.
  Summary: Cackle, a rooster who's
never seen a hen, comes home with
various unsuitable dates from a punkster
to a pig before finding the perfect mate.
  ISBN 0-87614-715-5
  [1. Roosters—Fiction. 2. Chickens—
Fiction. 3. Humorous stories.]
I. Rudebjer, Lars, 1958-   ill. II. Title.
PZ7.L65665Cac   1992
[E]—dc20   91-37338
                                           CIP
                                            AC

Manufactured in the
United States of America

1 2 3 4 5 6 7 8 9 10

01 00 99 98 97 96 95 94 93 92

Just as Cackle had said, Mother Tilda let him stay in the kitchen
the whole long, cold winter, along with his new wife (and family),
all twenty-three of them.

Cackle never felt like wandering anymore—which was a good
thing. For the old fox had certainly not forgotten Cackle and the
now-so-plump hens.